Dancing Pink Flamingos

and other Stories

Dancing Pink Flamingos and other Stories

MARIA TESTA

LERNER PUBLICATIONS COMPANY MINNEAPOLIS

Library of Congress Cataloging-in-Publication Data
Testa, Maria.
  Dancing pink flamingos and other stories/by Maria Testa.
    p. cm.
  Contents: Dancing pink flamingos—The Yale girl—The corrupting of Fouad—A cousin thing—Family day—Math genius—A good deal—Facing Donegall Square—Rock star—Immortality.
  Summary: A collection of short stories about young people in a variety of urban situations and settings.
  ISBN 0-8225-0738-2
  1. Children's stories, American. [1. City and town life—Fiction. 2. Short stories.] I. Title.
PZ7.T2877Dan 1995
[Fic]—dc20   95-4105

Manufactured in the United States of America
1 2 3 4 5 6 – BP – 00 99 98 97 96 95

For Mom, with love

CONTENTS

DANCING PINK FLAMINGOS

SAL LOMBARDI WALKS DOWN THE center aisle of the cathedral, places a white rose on Domenic's coffin, and all I can think is how much I hate him. I glance at my sister sitting next to me, and she squeezes my hand, knowing. Teresa is the one who first said that Sal looks like the kind of guy who has pink flamingos dancing all over his front lawn. No class.

I stare at Sal as he heads back to his pew. He just can't make himself wear a tie, not even today. His shirt collar is wide open so that God and everyone can see his gold chain. At a glance, you might think he's wearing a crucifix or something, but if you take a closer look you can tell that it's really a little gold karate guy doing some kind of flying kick. That's Sal Lombardi. He was Domenic's karate teacher. He taught Domenic all about being a "man." I'm so glad Sal could make it to the funeral.

The Mass is over, and Teresa slips her arm around my waist as we leave the cathedral.

"You can do it, babe," she whispers, and the onslaught begins. I am surrounded by old and middle-aged Italian woman who pat my cheek and say, "Poor Silvia, honey," over and over again, and I feel like a widow at seventeen, even though Domenic and I were only together a year and a half and we broke up a month before he died. *Before.* He's been dead for four days, and it's already difficult to remember Before.

I'm just starting to think that maybe I'll get through all of this when Mickey, one of Domenic's loud friends, steps right into my path. His coal-black hair is slicked back in a ponytail, and the diamond stud in his ear glistens as he sneers at me.

"He loved you, you bitch," he says, and I ignore him and stare at the diamond while Teresa gets in his face. I don't know how she takes care of him, but she does.

Sal Lombardi climbs in the limo with Domenic's

mother and grandmother, and I want to scream. Who does he think he is? If he hadn't filled Domenic's head with all that macho karate garbage, maybe Domenic wouldn't have thought that losing his job and losing me were assaults on his manhood and the end of the world.

"Come on, babe, let's go straight to the house," Teresa says, and she gently cups my elbow and steers me to her car, smiling and nodding at all the appropriate people. Teresa is good in situations like this.

We pull up in front of Domenic's house, and my stomach sinks a little further when I see all the cars. I don't know how I'm going to deal with all those people. I'm glad Teresa is with me, but when we walk through the front door and all conversation stops dead, I want to run away, run anywhere, just run.

Teresa and I offer to help out in the kitchen, but Domenic's aunt Lena sees me and comes rushing over.

"Go on," I say to Teresa, "I can handle this alone."

Aunt Lena is a tall, beautiful woman who looks as if she could take control of any situation. The look is deceiving. She grasps my face in both of her hands and begins to cry.

"Poor little Silvia," she says. "Poor Domenic. How

could it have happened? Didn't he know the speed limit? Why would he drive so fast?"

Domenic's mother hears her, and she comes over and hugs me and Aunt Lena. She lacks her sister's good looks, but her strength is for real. Her eyes are red, but she is composed.

"Domenic wasn't driving that fast, Lena," she explains. "The road was new to him, and it was too dark, and he couldn't see the curve up ahead. It was an accident."

I want to shake both of them. Keep saying it! I want to scream. Keep saying it, and maybe someday you'll really believe it. Domenic wasn't stupid, and he wasn't reckless. *"Slow down, baby,"* he used to say when I was driving, when I was talking, when I was making plans. I want to tell them that Domenic didn't have accidents. But instead I hug them back and hear myself talking about how wonderful and smart and sensitive Domenic was.

Mickey and his idiot sidekick, J.J., join us and hug both of the older women. They even hug me, too. The two of them are dressed in black from head to toe, black ties on black shirts, everything black except Mickey's diamond. J.J. doesn't have a diamond yet, but it's only a matter of time. Mickey asks Domenic's mother if they can borrow me for a while.

They lead me across the room, and I don't even care.

"He loved you," Mickey says again. "If you stuck around a little longer he would've been able to handle everything, you bitch."

I don't know why, but I try to explain.

"We talked everything out," I say. "Domenic agreed with everything. We talked about things you guys wouldn't even understand." Like love, I continue silently. Like love and growing apart and entering different worlds.

"Oh, I understand," Mickey says. "You're going off to college, and you're too embarrassed to be seen with some high school dropout."

"Bitch," J.J. adds, reaching the outer limits of his vocabulary.

That's not it, I want to explain, but I know it's no use. I hear Sal Lombardi's laugh reverberate throughout the house, and I hate him so much it hurts.

"I've got to go to the bathroom," I say, and I brush past the guys, suddenly in a hurry.

I stare at myself in the bathroom mirror.

"Bitch," I whisper. "Bitch, bitch, bitch. Who do you think you are?"

I stare at my overmoussed, too-black hair. I stare

at the thick black liner under my eyes. I stare at the dark red lipstick, the streaks of pink blush, the scarlet press-on nails.

"You're different," I say out loud, but staring back at me is just another guido-chick, another girl from the neighborhood, and I don't think I know her.

I check my underpants and am almost relieved when I see the bright red stain. An excuse. It'll get me out of here for a while.

I find Teresa in the kitchen, washing dishes.

"I just got my period," I tell her. "Can I borrow your car to go home and change? I'll be right back."

"Of course," she says, and I dig the keys out of her handbag.

I'm almost out the front door when I hear a voice behind me.

"Hey, honey, do you think maybe you could give me a ride home?"

I turn around and almost die. Sal Lombardi.

Something happens and I can't say no, and the next thing I know I'm sitting in Teresa's car with Sal Lombardi and he's telling me to put the windshield wipers on, it's starting to rain.

I have absolutely nothing to say to this man—nothing civil, at least—and I am silent as I speed through the neighborhood. I can't get rid of him fast enough. Sal, for his part, doesn't seem to have much to say to me, either, except for pointing out an occasional left or right. His house isn't too far away, and we get there quickly. I stop at the foot of the driveway, but he doesn't get out. He turns to face me.

"Silvia," he says. "I know you don't like me too much, but there's something I got to tell you."

I have no idea how Sal knows how I feel about him, but I can't look him in the eye. I stare at the little karate guy dangling in his chest hair.

"You meant the world to Domenic. He loved you to death," Sal says, not exactly choosing his words carefully. "Don't feel too bad about the stuff his friends are saying. They're good guys, but they don't understand what you and Dom had."

I think he's really trying hard, so I manage to lift my head and look at his face. His eyes are soft.

"Thank you," I say.

"No." Sal holds up his hand. "I'm not finished." He shifts in his seat, and I almost leap out of the car when he reaches over to hold my hand.

"Sorry," he says, but he doesn't let go. "I just want you to know that Dom knew you were different. He knew it wasn't going to last." He stops and looks around, searching for words. "I mean, Dom loved you so much, he didn't want to hold you back."

I can feel Domenic now, feel him inside me, and I pull my hand away and hug myself tightly.

Sal steps out of the car, but leans back in again before closing the door.

"Get out," he says. "More than anything, Dom wanted you to get out of this place. Go to college. You can do it." He closes the door gently, and I watch him walk up the driveway and go inside.

The rain has dotted the windshield and my eyes are blurred with tears, but somehow I can see clearly. There they are, a whole flock of pink flamingos, high-stepping all over Sal Lombardi's lawn. I wonder why they look so beautiful.

THE
YALE
GIRL

HE WASN'T GOING TO MUG ANYBODY.
It was Friday afternoon and the sidewalk
was crowded, but they were walking three
across, almost in step, like a moving wall.
James glanced at Tass and Mac, trying to
follow their eyes, hoping they hadn't already
picked a target. What a team. He and Tass were
both tall and a little too skinny, and in between
them was Mac, that short and stocky and crazy
white clown. James didn't think Tass or Mac would
actually mug anybody, either, but with those two,
you could never be sure about anything.

They were playing their game, the Chapel Street

game, and judging from the wide berth everyone else on the street was giving them, they were playing it pretty well. The premise was that they hated Chapel Street and all of the Yale people on it. The object was to pick a target and stare, to make a move, to let some Yale type think you were going to mug him. James hated it. He hated games without rules.

The truth was, James liked Chapel Street. It was kind of a pretty street—about as pretty as a street could get in New Haven—with shops and restaurants on one side and tall Gothic buildings on the other. It was especially pretty when the winter afternoon turned to evening, and snow flurries had just begun to fall. But Mac ruined it by wanting to play the game.

James shook his head, embarrassed. He was always having weird thoughts, dreamy thoughts. Tass and Mac would laugh themselves into the hospital if they knew. James shoved his hands into his jeans pockets, pretending to pick a target, pretending to stare, secretly watching snowflakes dance under the streetlights.

But Mac was watching something else, and it was no secret. He grabbed James's arm.

"Look at that!" he said. He grinned his crazy grin, the one that always put James on guard immediately. But this time, James liked what he saw.

Right in front of them, about thirty feet away, was a girl. She was tall, with long, dark hair, and she looked real good in her black coat and sparkling silver earrings. She stopped and eyed them warily.

"Baby, I love you!" Mac sang off-key as he ran toward her with outstretched arms.

"Move, sweetheart," she said. She glared at Mac with piercing black eyes before lowering her head and ducking around him. She kept going, staring at James and Tass, daring them to say something. James froze. She brushed past him; startled, he practically jumped backward to get out of her way.

"Wow! What a live one!" Mac was bobbing and weaving like a boxer after a knockdown. He loved getting a reaction—any reaction—out of a girl.

"Shut up," James said, but he wasn't really angry. He just wanted Mac to be quiet, for once, so he could watch that girl walk swiftly down the street. He liked the way she moved.

Tass stamped the snow off his feet. "Come on," he said. "Leave her alone. Let's pick someone else."

"Wait, wait a minute." James waved him off with his hand. He watched the girl step into the card shop, half a block away. "I'll be right back," he said. He couldn't believe it himself, but he followed her.

"What am I doing?" James whispered as he all but pressed his nose against the card shop window.

She was in there, all right. She was talking to a short girl with close-cropped hair, and they were both waving their hands all over the place. It didn't take much to figure out they were real women, way older than sixteen.

James watched them, staring and thinking. He liked the way the tall one had glared at Mac. Most people on the street would relax just a bit when they saw Mac's white face with him and Tass, but this girl seemed to know that Mac was the crazy one, the one who might be dangerous. She seemed to know.

Ice-cold hands grabbed James around the throat and he thought he was dead.

"Let's *go!*" a voice roared into his ear. Tass. Mac was behind him, giggling like a hyena. Tass wrapped an arm around James's waist and half-dragged, half-carried him away from the window.

"My buddy, James, here," Mac announced at the top of his lungs to everyone on the street, "is in love with a Yale girl!"

He laughed loudly, too loudly, but James didn't care, not even when Tass joined in. They pushed and shoved each other up the street as people dodged to get out of their way. James didn't care if Tass and Mac laughed their heads off, and he didn't care if everyone on Chapel Street stared at him. He knew something none of them knew: just before

Tass dragged him away, the Yale girl had glanced up at the window. She smiled at him.

It didn't take long for James to conquer Chapel Street. He felt like he owned it. Sometimes he hung out there with Tass and Mac, or just with Tass, but most of the time, he hung out there alone. Alone was the best. Alone, James could be anybody, strolling down the street, gazing at window displays, buying a cup of French roast or hazelnut or the coffee of the day. Alone, after school, he could do whatever he wanted and think about whatever and whomever he wanted without anyone laughing or trying to get him to play the game. Alone was the way James liked it. And one day Tass figured that out.

James knew Tass was following him. It was another Friday afternoon on Chapel Street, and as usual, the sidewalk was crowded, but James knew Tass was back there, watching. James stopped in his tracks and turned, catching Tass by surprise. They stared at each other.

James was the first to speak. "Bored yet?" he asked.

Tass grinned. "Out of my mind. I never knew you were so boring. So. Find her yet?"

"Who?"

"The Yale girl." Tass didn't mind getting right to the point. "We know you're looking for her."

James shook his head. "Don't know what you're talking about. I'm not looking for anybody. I'm just hanging out, that's all. I'm not doing anything. You saw me. I'm not looking for anybody." Shut *up*, James ordered himself. Talk about overkill.

Tass couldn't even hide his disgust.

"Listen, J," he said, "just a little advice. Don't let her see you following her. She'll be dialing 911 in a minute."

"I'm not looking for her." James continued walking. Tass fell in step beside him. There was nothing else to say.

Three days later, James saw her.

It wasn't even on Chapel Street. He had just made a left off Chapel onto York and had gone maybe a block and a half, heading home, when he spotted her. She was crossing the street, coming from the corner store, carrying a couple of heavy-looking brown bags. She was headed for a big apartment building on James's side of the street. He was not about to miss this kind of opportunity. He broke into a jog and just beat her to the front door.

She seemed surprised to see him. James opened the door.

"Thank you!" She smiled. She studied him for a moment, and her smile widened. "So, how are you?"

James nodded. Nothing to say. She walked through the doorway, pausing to glance back over her shoulder.

"Thanks a lot, hon."

He let the door close behind her. She remembered him! Sure, she thought he was a kid—a kid who couldn't even talk—but she remembered him.

He headed back toward Chapel Street. It was in the opposite direction and was a longer way home, but James wanted to bask in his newfound glory while walking down his favorite street. It was perfect.

He jogged effortlessly up York Street, amazed at the power in his legs. He cut the corner onto Chapel sharply and slowed down. She remembered him. What a feeling.

He almost didn't see them, but they were pretty hard to miss. Four guys about his age, way out of place on Chapel Street, were walking right at him, staring. James tried not to laugh. He knew the game and he knew the score. In fact, he knew exactly what they were thinking and doing and even why they were there. He was sure of it.

It was only when a cold, hard fist crashed into the bridge of his nose, shooting rods of pain throughout his skull, shattering his thoughts, that James realized he still didn't know the rules.

THE
CORRUPTING
OF FOUAD

IT WAS THE BEGINNING OF THE
second month of the war with Iraq when
Diana noticed that her work had become
ugly. With a flick of a paintbrush, she
turned white canvasses into mud. Artists
were supposed to suffer during wartime, she told
herself, but she remained unconvinced. She did
not feel the war; it was simply out there, somewhere
far away. Diana watched the nightly televised bom-
bardment of Iraqi soil by American artillery, and
she felt nothing. It was not real. She could only
stare at the reality of her muddy canvasses and wonder when the ugliness would come to an end.

The library could provide the cure. At least, that's what Mr. Golini said. Mr. Golini was the only art teacher in the world who could have convinced Ms. Mendez, the principal at JFK High, to let Diana spend her fourth period study hall at the public library for a whole week. Her assignment was a written research project on the "ugly" periods of Picasso, Matisse, and Cézanne. It was supposed to be fun.

All the masters went through an ugly period, Mr. Golini had insisted, and the public library could offer Diana an understanding of their successes and failures. The school library was simply inadequate. And furthermore, the public library could provide her with the solitude every artist craves. That's what Mr. Golini argued, and it worked—at least on Ms. Mendez. Diana wasn't so sure. But she welcomed the opportunity to escape from school, if only for one period, and if only to Mr. Golini's beloved public library.

Diana expected five days of books, paintings, and inspiration. She did not expect Fouad.

She was lost in Matisse, and everything was beautiful. Diana sat alone at an isolated table in the back of the art section of the library—every Matisse book in the place stacked in front of her—and she was overwhelmed. Color surrounded her. Pure, perfect color. The man never experienced an ugly day in his life. Diana leaned back in her chair and ran her fingers through her long, black hair. This isn't inspiring, she thought, this is depressing. And it was only Monday.

"Are you an Arab?"

She looked up, startled. What a weird question. Diana wasn't sure if she had really heard it.

"Excuse me. Are you an Arab?"

Okay, she really did hear it that time, and the voice was coming from somewhere behind her. She turned in her seat and stared into a pair of brown eyes as dark as her own.

"No," she said to the most beautiful boy in the world. "I'm sorry. I'm Italian." Diana wondered why she was apologizing.

The boy nodded, as if it all made sense. "Well, I am Fouad, and I'm an Arab," he said.

He held up a book of Islamic art as evidence. He slid into the chair next to Diana's, placed his book on the table, and turned to her, hugging his knees.

"My name's Diana," she said, not quite sure if he was listening.

"Don't you want to know what kind of Arab I am, Diana?" Fouad asked. So he was listening, after all.

It was a great feeling, being a step behind a kid who was probably all of eleven.

"Okay," she said. "What kind of an Arab are you?"

"Iraqi." It was an announcement. "I am an Iraqi." He tapped his book gently. "Do you know where the capital of Islamic art is?"

Diana was starting to feel like an actor playing an assigned role. Still, she was intrigued enough to comply.

"Where?"

"Baghdad," he said. He sat up straight in his chair, opened his book, and began to read. Conversation over.

Diana turned back to Matisse. Colors danced and blurred before her eyes as she stole quick glances at Fouad. He was adorable, but he was also a pretty strange little kid. His black T-shirt was so long it could have been a dress, despite the fluorescent orange letters screaming the name of some metal band Diana had never heard of.

"Do you think Baghdad is still standing?"

Diana sat up straight. The questions were getting tougher. Fouad wasn't even looking at her; he seemed to be talking to the printed page in front of him.

Diana decided to answer, anyway. "I don't really know," she said carefully. "I do know that there has been a lot of bombing. I'm sure there's quite a bit of damage."

"It's a big city, you know," Fouad said. "I was there once. We were visiting my grandmother. There are a lot of people there." He had turned to Diana again and was speaking very quickly. He reached over to open the Matisse book and, with one finger, gently began to trace the twisting lines of *Promenade Among the Olive Trees.*

"Do you like the painting?" Diana asked.

"It's pretty," he said. "Do you paint like this?"

"Not quite." She tried to keep a straight face. Not in this lifetime, honey, she thought. "But I try."

"So do I," Fouad said. "I like to paint. Art is important." He averted his eyes, suddenly shy. "Will you be here tomorrow?" he asked.

Diana smiled. "Same time. Same place."

"I'm working on a painting at home," he said. "Can I show it to you tomorrow?"

"Sure, but don't you have to be in school?"

Fouad shook his head. "We're moving in a week," he explained. "To California. My dad says I don't have to go to school until we get there."

"That's great." Diana gathered up her books. "I'll see you tomorrow, then." She glanced at her watch. Where did the time go? She hadn't accomplished anything.

"Um, Diana?" Fouad was standing right by her side. "Can I ask you one more thing?" He didn't wait for a response. "Are you a good artist?"

The kid knew how to ask a difficult question, that was for sure.

"I think so," Diana said. "But right now I'm going through a difficult period."

"That's funny," Fouad said, his voice almost a whisper. "So am I."

"Mama says it's ugly."

Fouad shifted his backpack and tentatively handed a posterboard to Diana. She wondered how long he had been there, waiting for her alone in the art section. She unrolled the poster carefully and stared. Mama was wrong.

Diana sat down at the nearest table. She could definitely teach this kid a thing or two about ugly. Ugly was not one of his problems.

"Fouad," Diana said after a moment. "Did you paint this all by yourself?"

"Yes," he said, "but that's the problem. I don't want to finish it alone." He smiled an endearing smile. "I want you to work on it with me. Please."

Please. He said please. It was almost funny. Diana was flattered that he wanted to paint with her— maybe even intimidated. She studied the figures on the posterboard. Fouad was no realist, but there was something hauntingly true about the faceless people in the painting, their arms and legs flailing wildly, heads tilted back toward the sky as if beseeching God or witnessing the destruction of heaven itself. The painting was so powerful Diana wanted to hide it, as if it might be dangerous.

"I would love to work with you," she said finally. "But Fouad, are you sure you want anyone to even touch this?"

"Yes," he insisted. "Just look at it. It's all in shades of gray. It needs color, and I haven't decided if I'm going to give the people faces or if I'm going to leave them blank."

They studied the painting together, sharing ideas.

"Color will work," Diana said. "I can help you with that. But you're going to have to make the final decision about faces on your own. That's too important."

Fouad emptied his backpack onto the table. Small tubes of acrylic paint and well-worn brushes bounced across the surface and onto the floor. He was ready to begin, right there in the art section of the library. An appropriate place to paint, Diana thought. The art section was so secluded, no one would even notice.

"So, you really like the painting?" Fouad asked,

grinning. Diana picked up a paintbrush and twirled it like a baton.

"Fouad, I think I'm in love with it."

After painting with Fouad for the next couple of days, Diana knew she was in over her head. Not artistically, really, although she had to admit that she was well challenged to match the little fauve brushstroke for brushstroke. It was a question of content and context; she could deal with how Fouad was working and creating, but she was afraid of why.

The more they painted, and the more they added color and life to the work, the more the intuition Diana was trying to suppress was confirmed: Baghdad was burning, and she was watching it go up in flames.

Fouad was waiting for her again on Friday.

"Do you think we'll finish today?" He seemed excited, even more energetic than usual. "I still haven't decided about the faces. Which way should we go?"

Diana didn't know what to do about the faces. For some reason, she didn't feel like painting at all. And she didn't know why she said what she said: "Fouad, let's not paint today. Let's go for a walk in the park, instead." It was cold outside, freezing. Who could possibly want to go for a walk in the park?

"The park?" Fouad was surprised at first, then thrilled. "Why not? Let's go for a walk in the park!"

They walked and talked—about the painting, mostly. Diana wondered why they never really talked about much else. It seemed odd, now that she thought about it. She dragged her feet through the slush and dirty snow while Fouad stopped frequently to make slush balls. He threw them at various targets, including Diana. She got a little wetter than she had planned, but she wasn't annoyed. It was nice to see Fouad acting like a little kid.

She didn't hear any sirens. She didn't see any flashing blue or red lights, either. If she had, maybe Diana wouldn't have walked right into the large male cop who suddenly blocked their path.

"Fouad Hassan!" The cop's voice seemed unnaturally loud. He was staring at Fouad, who gazed past him, refusing to look him in the eye.

"What's going on?" Diana tried to control her voice, to keep it from rising. The cop grabbed her left arm above the elbow; not roughly, but it wasn't exactly a caress, either.

"Who the hell are you?" was all he said. It wasn't a question. If he wanted to shut her up, all he had to do was tell her to shut up. Fouad seemed to have no intention of saying anything. The cop led them to his car in silence.

"Where are we going?" Diana asked after they had been driving for four or five minutes. It took her that long to get up the nerve to speak again.

"The station. The kid's parents are there." The cop glanced at Diana in the rearview mirror, and their eyes met. She hoped a little human contact would permit her to ask another question.

"Did something happen?"

"Well, why don't you just tell me!" He slammed his hand against the steering wheel. "I'm out looking for a missing juvenile and what do I find? A kidnapping? The corrupting of a minor? I don't like what I'm seeing, but you're not exactly a typical felon, either, honey."

"A felon? Me?" Diana felt herself losing it, about to go on the offensive. "*I'm* a minor!" she shouted. "Am I under arrest, or what?"

"Relax," the cop said. He sounded almost apologetic. "Nobody's under arrest."

"Fouad and I are friends," Diana said, her jaw clenched. "We're artists, and we talk about art." She turned to Fouad, who was staring out the window, watching the city go by. "Go ahead, Fouad. Tell him."

Nothing. The cop was looking in the rearview mirror again. Diana caught him studying her before he quickly averted his eyes.

"Uh, miss," he said slowly. "The parents say the

kid doesn't talk." Fouad continued to stare out the window in silence.

Diana wanted to shake him, but she felt weak. Her head was pounding. She closed her eyes, trying to block out everyone and everything around her.

"The kid," she said, "doesn't shut up."

Diana learned a lot at the police station. Fouad's family never had plans to move to California. Fouad did not have his father's permission to skip school. In fact, his parents weren't even aware that he hadn't been in school for more than two weeks, until the vice principal had called them that very morning with the news.

"It's the war," his father explained over and over. "It's the war. He hasn't said a word in a month."

There was a lot Diana didn't learn, too, a lot she couldn't even begin to understand. But Ms. Mendez had come through for her; after one phone call, the police were satisfied that she was an innocent player in the whole saga. Mr. Golini arrived at the station to take her back to school. Diana practically collapsed into his arms.

"What happened, Diana?" he said, patting her back as if she were the lost child.

"I don't know," she said, trying not to cry. "Let's just get out of here."

"Diana, wait." Mr. Golini gestured behind her.

It was Fouad, alone. He was clutching the rolled posterboard too tightly, but his eyes were calm, even serene.

"Diana," he said, "I have decided. They need to have faces. All of the people need to have faces." He handed the painting to her and was gone.

Back at school, alone in the art studio, Diana agreed. She mixed paints instinctively. She played with the colors on her palette, thinking. She thought of Fouad and his talent and promise. She thought of the day, of the police station, of guilt, and of silence. She thought a lot about silence, and, at last, she was ready to paint.

She painted well past school hours. Mr. Golini looked in on her once, but simply smiled and did not speak. Diana painted until everyone had a face, until everyone had an expression, until there was only one thing left to say.

"I'm sorry, Fouad," she said out loud. And then she said it again and again until the words seemed to bounce off the studio walls and speak in a voice of their own.

I'm sorry, Fouad. I'm sorry.

Diana held up the painting before her, and she knew that it was beautiful.

A
Cousin
Thing

MOST PEOPLE ARE KIND OF SUR-
prised when they find out I stabbed a
guy, once. I can't really blame them. I
mean, I look pretty normal. They're even
more surprised when they find out it happened when I was just thirteen and in eighth
grade. When it happened, I still had my backpack
slung over my shoulder with my uniform skirt
stuffed in it. I don't think the guy was really hurt,
although I never found out for sure. He had a
leather jacket on, and it was pretty thick.

The day started off normally enough, but I knew
something was up. My cousin, Anita, said she'd pick

me up after school, which wasn't weird or anything, but it was unusual. I used to see Anita a couple of times a month, usually at family parties or funerals or things like that. She was sixteen and didn't bother with me too much. She certainly never picked me up from school before.

She told me not to tell my mother. This should have been my first clue, because Anita always said I had the coolest mom in the world. So all during the school day, I felt like I was up to something, like I had something to hide. I was preoccupied. I mean, I didn't even care when Sister Mary Maureen Murphy (that's her real name, but we called her Sister Mo) told me I was slipping in math. Usually it would tick me off when she said something like that because it wasn't true. I just didn't pay attention all the time, that's all. If I wasn't paying attention, even I could get something wrong sometimes. It didn't mean I had suddenly become stupid.

When the day finally ended and Anita picked me up, I didn't know what to expect. I was pretty cool about it, though. I didn't ask any questions until I had already pulled on my jeans and whipped off my skirt. I'm really good at changing clothes in a moving car. Everyone who ever went to my school is. You kind of had to be. I mean, after around sixth grade, you really don't want to be seen in public wearing your "I'm-a-nice-Catholic-schoolgirl" skirt. Most of the time, it's better to be a little more anonymous than that.

As a general rule, when you're in uniform, no guy you might be interested in will ever talk to you. But all these other guys—especially older ones, like over twenty or something—will think you're the cutest thing on earth. I don't get it, but that's just the way it is. So you keep a pair of jeans in your backpack and you learn how to change in the car.

Anyway, it ended up that I only had to ask Anita one question. I brought it up, and she took off from there. No, we were not going to her house, we were going to Nick's school. Nick was our cousin and a senior, and he went to Jefferson, which was the biggest high school in the city. It was supposed to be wild, and it fascinated me. I'd heard all kinds of stories about what went on there, like people dealing drugs in the back of classrooms and having sex in the maintenance closets. I don't know if any of this stuff was true or not, but the graffiti on the outside of the building was proof enough for me. Let's just say it was pretty creative. Every time I read it, I learned a new word.

So we were supposed to meet Nick and five or six more cousins in the parking lot behind Jefferson, depending on who showed. Anita said if we were lucky, some of Nick's friends would be hanging around, too. We might need them. I began to understand that it was all about Tommy.

Nick's brother Tommy had gotten himself messed up with crack. It seemed like he got into it overnight. From what I hear, sometimes that's all it takes. Our whole family was going a little crazy about Tommy because everyone thought something really bad might happen. I don't know if anyone was doing anything to help him or if anybody even knew how. Then Anita started talking about some dealer, and I knew right away we were in over our heads. Nick wanted to lean on some guy he was convinced was turning Tommy into an addict.

Now Nick was just about the biggest seventeen-year-old in the world, but I still thought the whole thing sounded absolutely idiotic. Anita said that's why she wanted me to come along. I was level-headed, and besides, Nick adored me. I was pretty crazy about him, too. He had dark curly hair and the best little scar over his left eyebrow. He was definitely the kind of guy you wouldn't want to be caught dead wearing your uniform around. And Nick always said I was scary smart, which I took as a compliment. I don't know, I guess it was kind of a cousin thing.

It was Anita's idea that I carry Nick's knife. I was

the youngest and least likely to have it, and nobody wanted Nick to actually use it. I agreed. But when we all met up at Jefferson I told Nick that I thought the whole thing was idiotic, and he said I was probably right. Anyway, nothing was going to happen. Just a lot of talk, that's all. All we wanted to do was cut off the supply, just cut off the supply.

Nick asked me if I would rather sit in Anita's car at the other end of the parking lot and wait for her there. I knew he couldn't believe that Anita brought me along. After all, I was only thirteen and a kid. But there was no way I was going to sit in that car alone. I stayed by Anita's side.

Well, this dealer guy showed up and he looked like he was barely old enough to even go to Jefferson, but he brought about fifty million of his friends, and we were so outnumbered I thought we were all going to die. Nick was right, there was a lot of talk. There was a lot of talk, and pushing, and shoving, and screaming, and then all hell broke loose. Finally, there was a knife sticking straight up out of a guy's shoulder. It was Nick's knife. I didn't even know who the guy was. All I remember is the leather jacket, especially the skull and crossbones on the back. It wasn't the type of thing you forget.

We ran. There were too many drug dealer types between us and the car, so we just ran like hell. Now that I think about it, we definitely made a mistake by running down sidewalks, in full view of everyone, like it would have been against somebody's rules to step off the curb. We should have cut through alleys, yards, parking lots. We really should have.

It's pretty tough to outrun a police car; something about those swirling blue lights just seems to slow down your legs. And then, when another police car came at us from the front, we knew we were caught. "We" were me and Anita and her sister, Lisa, and another cousin, Natalie, and we—not exactly the toughest crowd the cops ever faced—were scared. All of us. I knew I wasn't the only one.

Anita kind of took charge from there. She told us to stop and just sit on the curb, right there in front of some old warehouse. We're girls, she said, just sweet, innocent little girls, so act it. We sat there on that curb, four in a row. If I'd had some chalk in my pocket, I swear I would have drawn squares for hopscotch.

The cops didn't buy the innocent act, but they weren't too thrilled that they only caught up with us girls. We didn't know where the guys were or what happened to them, and we were glad we didn't. I wasn't about to narc on any of my cousins.

But then the cops started staring at me. At first, I almost died. *They know!* I thought. *How did they know?* The guy in the leather jacket never even saw me, I was sure of it.

One of the cops smiled down at me and held out both of his hands like he wanted to help me stand up. Don't be scared, honey, he said, or something like that. I got up on my own. He put his hand on my shoulder and sort of steered me toward the back of his car, still smiling. He asked me how old I was as if I was about five, but that was okay. It was good to be young, and if I knew anything, it was how to be thirteen. When the cop actually picked me up and sat me down on the car trunk, I knew everything was going to be fine, just fine. He didn't know anything. I was in control.

I talked. I mean, I practically sang. I told him all about my day, about math class and Sister Mo, about Anita picking me up after school. I took off my backpack and showed him my uniform skirt, and then I told him all about my crush on my big cousin, Nick. I told him my whole life story and maybe even more, until he stopped listening and had long since stopped smiling, and I was pretty sure that cop never wanted to hear me say another word, ever again. I told him everything. I just left out the part about Nick's knife. It was a cousin thing.

FAMILY
DAY

I WAS THIRTEEN WHEN MY FATHER was arrested, fourteen when his case came to trial, and fifteen when he was sentenced, following a failed appeal. When the judge finally closed the books on our family's long encounter with the American system of criminal justice, I was nothing but relieved. Five years in prison, I figured, was long enough for any guy to forget what his father's face looked like. I welcomed the opportunity. My mother, however, had other ideas.

Sundays were family days, Mamma insisted, and

family days they would remain. After only three months of spending most of every Sunday in federal prison, I was tired of the whole scene. Saturdays were mine, Mamma promised me that, but my one day of freedom was tainted by the prospect of yet another Sunday looming ahead. My little brother, Ralphie, celebrated his eighth birthday on a Sunday, in prison. Sunday afternoon football games became a thing of the past.

Every Sunday, after eight o'clock Mass, Mamma would rummage through her closet and emerge with a makeshift outfit that never met with her approval. She would stand in front of the bathroom mirror and apply colorful creams and powders to her face, shaking her head at the results. Each and every Sunday, Mamma would struggle through this appearance-altering ritual in an attempt to achieve some undefined standard of prison-wife beauty. She wanted to please him, but I never saw her smile at her own reflection.

It was the first Sunday of December—the fifth month of the first year—when Ralphie decided to take matters into his own hands. From the beginning he had approached our prison visits as something of a challenge, but this day was somehow different. It all started in the waiting room.

The waiting room is hell. I suppose this is true of the waiting room in any prison, but I only know about our prison. They should probably call it the Eternal Waiting Room From Hell, because on Sunday, you have to wait for an eternity. I guess every mother in the world shares Mamma's view of Sundays; the waiting room was always filled with families. We all had to wait for hours in something resembling a line—sitting, standing, and leaning, kids crying, everybody shouting, nobody really talking.

"Let's talk," Daddy says, as we flop on the grass in the backyard. "It's good for a father and son to talk." I smile and close my eyes as the sun warms my face. It's Sunday afternoon, and I'm wearing new jeans and a red baseball cap.

"So, tell me, Anthony," Daddy says. "What are your plans for tomorrow?" I laugh because he already knows. It's spring, and baseball tryouts are tomorrow. Daddy and I have been practicing every Sunday afternoon for the last six weeks. Most of the other kids at tryouts will be eleven or twelve years old. But Daddy says I'm going to make it even though I'm only nine.

"I'm ready, Daddy," I say. "I'm going to be the best shortstop in the whole league."

"Go for it, Anthony, baby," he says, and he flicks my cap down over my eyes.

e

A guard pointed to the baseball cap I was wear-ing backwards, like I always did.

"Lose it," he said, and I pulled it off and stuffed it in the back pocket of my jeans. I don't know why the guards cared, but they never let me keep my cap on very long.

When we finally reached the front of the line after the usual two-and-a-half hour wait, it was time to begin the admittance rituals. Mamma had to fill out some forms, and all three of us, even Ralphie, had to sign the visitors' log. A guard searched Mamma's handbag, and then we had to walk through the metal detector. We usually breezed through this part with no problem. Usually. But this Sunday, Ral-phie had a little trouble making it through.

The alarm was almost deafening. Mamma was bending over, searching Ralphie's pockets, when I realized what was going on. When the guard told Ralphie to walk back through again, he still set the thing off. I caught Ralphie's eye and smiled at him in confidence.

"Nickels in your shoes?" I asked in a stage whisper.

Ralphie raised his eyebrows and grinned as wickedly as any eight-year-old can, and when the alarm went off once again, the guard himself searched my brother. Ralphie voluntarily took off his left shoe, triumphantly revealing two bright red toy magnets. The guard was not impressed. Mamma frowned.

"I forgot," Ralphie said, falling back on a little-kid excuse he didn't expect anyone to believe.

I rolled my eyes. The guard scowled. Mamma turned her head and smiled.

We dutifully held out our right hands, three in a row, and a second guard stamped them. I watched the image of a V on my hand dry until it was invisible, like it was supposed to be. Ralphie licked his hand and grimaced.

"Don't try it," he advised. I had to give the kid credit. He seemed determined to make the day at least somewhat interesting.

The three of us finally got through the automatic double doors that separated the waiting room from the visiting room. I sort of liked how they worked. One door wouldn't open until the other was completely closed. And when that second door closes behind you—not with the clang of an old movie, but with the dull thud of reality—believe me, you know you are in prison.

Mamma handed the necessary papers verifying who we were and all that to the desk guard, a woman I had never seen before. She was dressed just like all the men, with a tie and everything, including one of those tie clips that looks like tiny handcuffs. The tie clip must have been an official part of the uniform; all the guards wore one. Maybe it was some kind of private joke.

If the waiting room is hell, the visiting room is more like purgatory. Families are together, but not really. People seem happy to see each other, but not really. Little kids run in and out and all around the tables and chairs, laughing and playing, but not really. I had to fight the urge to run out there with those kids and show them how to really play, how to have fun. I used to know.

I'm the best athlete in the neighborhood, and Dad knows it. Sometimes I think he's kind of jealous. I'm down at the playground shooting hoops with some of the guys when Dad shows up, ready to play.

"Over here, Anthony, baby," he calls out, holding up his hands. I'm already embarrassed, but I toss the ball to him anyway. He snorts loudly and throws up an air ball. He takes out a handkerchief and blows his nose, but it's still running. Dad's been sick for weeks. I don't know why he's out here trying to prove himself to a bunch of seventh-graders.

Mamma put her hand on my shoulder and pointed across the room.

"See that nice table in the corner over there?" she asked. "Go ahead and save it so we can have some privacy."

I scanned the sea of mostly occupied, kindergartenesque white tables and orange chairs. Nice table? Privacy? The noise level alone was an invasion of privacy. I cut across the room and stood by the table. Mamma smiled and nodded.

Ralphie was off and running with some of his friends almost immediately. He really had friends there, and they were nice little kids. I would have liked them, too, if I were eight years old. Ralphie was actually something of a junior-league gang leader. He picked up a chair and held it over his head, barking orders at some other, more timid little kids. Mamma sat down and ignored him. I think she was embarrassed.

After a pretty typical fifteen-minute wait, my father entered the visiting room from the opposite end, through the door reserved for prisoners who had to be accompanied by guards, which was just about everybody except for the white-collar guys. Mamma spotted him right away, as she always did, and jumped out of her seat to meet him. Ralphie noticed right away, too. He dropped the chair he was carrying, raced over to our father, and grabbed him around the waist. Mamma embraced both of them.

My father grinned proudly over Mamma's shoulder and extended his right arm out toward me as I approached. He grabbed me by the back of the neck and messed up my hair.

"Getting to be quite a man there, Anthony, baby!" He pulled me closer.

After all the initial hugging and smiling and *miss yous*, Ralphie ran off with his friends again, and Mamma, my father, and I sat down at our table. We talked about family things and school and money. Eventually I dropped out of the conversation and sat back. Mamma and my father leaned closer together, talking quietly, and I didn't even try to listen. This was their private time, when they would kiss, and Mamma would trace the bones of my father's face with her fingers and lips. I never saw them like this when my father was home, and I didn't like it at all.

"Where have you been? Where have you been? Where have you been?" Mamma is shouting, and she's almost hysterical. My father walks right past her as if he hasn't been missing for three whole days, no explanation needed. He's dirty and unshaven and

looks like he hasn't slept at all. He probably doesn't need to. He's wired, shaking all over, and his nose is running down his face.

Mamma is on his heels, still shouting, but he doesn't give her a chance. The back of his hand flies through the air, and Mamma crashes into the wall. Ralphie throws himself to the floor, cowering next to her. I'm thirteen and almost a man and I do nothing.

My father started to caress Mamma's face, and I couldn't watch any longer. I tipped my chair back a bit and allowed my eyes to roam. All around me, people were kissing and touching, pretending they were alone. I was starting to get uncomfortable, and I glanced back at my own parents just in time to watch Ralphie try to kill our father.

He didn't succeed. I don't know what he was thinking; no eight-year-old could kill a grown man by smashing an orange plastic chair over his head. The chair did bounce off my father's left shoulder, though, loudly enough to attract the attention of most of the people sitting around us. Ralphie's screams attracted everyone else. He threw himself on the floor, bawling his head off, gasping for air. He was distraught about his failure.

People gathered around as Mamma knelt beside Ralphie, patting his cheek and trying to calm him.

My father stood over them with his back to me and his hands on his hips. The man was bewildered.

"What, is he crazy or something?" he asked anyone who would listen.

My chest hurt. I gazed over at my father's empty chair. The back was plastic, but the seat was reinforced with a solid sheet of metal. Ralphie, the poor kid, had hit our father with the plastic part.

He's only eight years old, I thought, as I turned to face my father's unsuspecting back, his chair held high over my head.

MATH
GENIUS

"PROFESSOR SCHMIDT IS WRONG," I say out loud, and my words reverberate throughout the empty stairwell with almost enough power to convince me of their truth.

I lean against the wall and raise my oboe to my lips, ready to play. I like practicing here. The practice studios in the music building are excellent by most people's standards, but I prefer the sound in the dormitory stairwell, the way every note bounces off the walls—almost developing an echo, but not quite—filling space and time and most importantly, my mind. This stairwell is my sanctuary.

My hallmates know I practice here. No one makes a big deal of it, really. Everyone basically understands that Cristina plays the oboe, and she likes to practice in the stairwell, and she likes to be there alone. It's an idiosyncrasy no one has any real trouble accepting since I'm otherwise normal and easy to live with.

I'm playing louder now, louder and faster, scales and exercises that have become automatic through the years, and I struggle to keep my mind from wandering. I try to think about music. I try to think about music and composition and performance, but I cannot stop myself from thinking about Professor Schmidt.

I barely know the man. Yesterday, I didn't even know he existed. The memo in my mailbox was clearly addressed to me, but the scribbled message seemed misdirected: "Please see me. Soon." Who was this Professor Schmidt, and why would he want to see me?

It was easy enough to find out. Back in the dorm, alone in my room, I flipped to the index of the First Year Guide and scanned the names under S. I found Schmidt, I read that he was the head of the Math Department, and I went cold.

I stumble over a scale, the final note ending in a scream, and my concentration is lost as the scream echoes in my head, hauntingly familiar. I allow my lips to relax and slide down the reed, and the stairwell is silent. But silence is the one thing I cannot handle, and I try to continue playing as Professor Schmidt's words interrupt my rhythm: "Math is related to music in many ways, Cristina. You should find time for both."

I do not want to find time for both. There is no choice; I have no options. I really start to play now, with controlled confidence and feeling, but as the music swells to fill the stairwell, I close my eyes and remember my past, not so very long ago, when I was a math genius.

"It's freezing. Let's go back inside," Karen said as we took our first step outside the hotel lobby. I glanced at Sam, who smiled and shrugged. He placed his hand on Karen's back and gave her a gentle-but-firm shove, which I'm sure she thoroughly enjoyed. Those two liked each other from the moment we all met at the train station in Providence, three Rhode Island math brains on our way to Yale to prove the depths of our genius.

"Okay!" Karen held up her hands and danced ahead of us. "But—promise me we'll be back in our rooms by noon? I really want to spend most of the day cramming."

"So do I," Sam said, "but we've got to eat. You know, brain food."

I didn't say anything. It was my idea that the three of us go to breakfast. I had never been to New Haven before, and I thought we could hang out and explore the Yale campus together. I had no plans to spend the day studying; I wasn't even remotely concerned about the exam tomorrow. I had never studied for a math exam in my life, and I wasn't about to start. But Sam and Karen seemed like pre-ulcer types—the kind who give math jocks a bad name. Well, at least they'd found each other.

Sam wrapped one arm around Karen and then pulled me over to wrap the other around me, like he thought I might be jealous or something. He held us close as we walked along, obviously enjoying himself.

"Won't it be great," he said, "if we all end up at MIT next year?" His enthusiasm was almost too much for me.

"Oh, I don't know," I said. "I might want to go to Yale. Or maybe someplace a little more laid-back, like Brown."

Sam and Karen both looked hurt, like I was rejecting them, which I guess I was. I felt kind of bad, especially because I was lying. I was definitely on my way to MIT.

"Come on, guys," I said, trying to explain. "There's more to life than math."

"Of course there is!" Now Karen was really insulted. "But if you're serious about mathematics, then MIT is the place to be."

I didn't want to argue. I pretty much agreed with her, anyway, and I was certainly serious about math. We crossed the street, and I stopped in front of a bookstore window.

"There's a diner a couple of blocks ahead, Cristina," Sam said. Karen shivered dramatically. So neither of them wanted to stop. I didn't care. I smiled.

"Why don't you two go ahead," I suggested. "I just want to look in this window for a minute. I'll catch up with you."

"Fine," Karen said loudly, overpowering Sam's attempt to ask me if I was sure.

"Yes, I'm sure," I said to Sam, anyway. I watched them walk up the street, not quite holding hands.

I turned to gaze at the bookstore window. Sam and Karen weren't bad, really. Sam was actually kind of good-looking in a sandy-haired, clean-cut sort of way. And he was definitely the sensitive type, which is always better than the alternative. Karen was okay, too, just a little uptight. Her short, light-brown hair was cut bluntly and precisely to chin length, and her pale blue jacket matched her eyes perfectly. Definitely a little uptight.

I smiled at my reflection. What did the all-American couple-to-be think of my mane of wild black corkscrew curls and taunting dark eyes? Be nice to them, I silently ordered my reflection, but I could not control the smile in the window.

I gazed up the street. Sam and Karen were a block ahead of me; it was time to break up their private party. I jogged after them, slowly but gaining steadily, until I was almost within calling distance. But I never got a chance to call out their names.

Suddenly I was sprawled on the sidewalk, the wind knocked out of me. It was a few seconds before I realized that I wasn't alone. On the ground, surrounding me, were four or five guys, kids really, two or three years younger than me.

"Wow! What a collision!" one of them said, grinning in my face. "Are you okay?" He helped me sit up.

I nodded, but I didn't dare speak. I was pretty sure I didn't even have a voice.

"That was really wild," the kid continued. "You were running up the street and we were running down it, and then all of a sudden...BAM!" He smacked his hands together. "Head-on collision!"

I think I smiled, but I still couldn't speak. Then I

saw my wallet, wide open on the sidewalk in front of us. It must have fallen out of my jacket pocket, I thought. The kid noticed it, too. He picked it up, and I held out my hands for him to give it back to me. He grinned sweetly as he dropped my wallet deep inside his coat pocket instead.

"Come on, guys, let's help her up," he called to his friends, and then I was on my feet. Sam and Karen were suddenly right there in front of me, reaching out as if they were afraid I might fall.

"My God, Cristina, what happened?" Sam looked genuinely concerned as he held me tightly. Karen looked scared half to death.

"She's okay," the kid with the coat said. "Just a little shook up, that's all." I stared at him. He was almost lost in that oversized black topcoat, like a child wearing his father's clothes.

"Well, thanks for helping her out," Sam said. He was so sincere, I wanted to scream. But I still couldn't make a sound.

"No problem." The kid flashed that sweet grin again, and he and his friends headed down the street, walking at first, but then breaking out into a full-fledged sprint.

"It was nice of them to help you up," Karen said, like she really meant it. Karen and Sam actually thought those kids had done me some kind of favor. I stared hard at both of them, first one, then the other.

"Those little bastards took my wallet," was all I said.

I was right about Sam: he was a truly sensitive guy. It was his idea that the three of us spend the rest of the morning in my hotel room, having a room-service breakfast. We sat on the bed, picnic-style, like three little kids at a slumber party. I never drank so much hot chocolate in my life, but I had to admit, it did help me feel better.

"I can't believe the police aren't going to do anything," Sam said for what must have been the twenty-eighth time.

I didn't want to call the police in the first place, but Sam had insisted. I knew that one synthetic leather wallet and twenty-three dollars in cash weren't going to be anyone's top priority, but even I didn't expect the cop on the phone to laugh my ear off. I guess your sense of humor gets kind of warped when you're dealing with gangs and crack and guns all day long. But Sam was still pretty indignant.

"I'm telling you," he continued, "I don't know who would want to go to Yale with stuff like this happening all the time."

It wasn't exactly the crime of the century—and I

was pretty sure "stuff like this" happened just as often at MIT—but for some reason, I didn't want to disagree. Sam was hovering, and it was kind of nice.

"Don't worry," I said. "I'm going to MIT. Honest. I am."

"Well, that's good," Karen said, but I didn't believe her for a minute. Something was happening here that Karen didn't like at all.

Sam glanced at his watch and started to pile the breakfast dishes back on the tray.

"Time to start studying?" I asked.

"I guess so," he said, "if you're sure you're all right."

"Hey, I'm fine, I mean it." I smiled, hoping he would believe me. I wasn't all that sure if I was fine or not. "I brought my oboe along, and I think I'll practice for a while."

Karen stared at me. "You're crazy if you don't study," she said. "A really high score tomorrow could guarantee you a scholarship to just about anywhere you want to go. It's an honor even to be chosen to take this exam."

I shrugged nonchalantly, because I knew it would annoy her.

"I don't think I'm crazy," I said.

"And neither do I." Sam smiled at both of us. "You're just different, that's all." He swung his legs over the side of the bed and stood up. "Come on, Karen," he said. "Let's leave the musician to her oboe. I know that I, for one, definitely need to study."

I walked them to the door, suddenly aware that the last thing in the world I wanted was to be alone.

"Come back and visit any time you guys want a break," I said. I could only hope I didn't sound too pathetic.

They weren't gone five minutes when I heard a knock on the door. I rushed to open it. Sam. I was pleasantly not-very-surprised.

We sat on the edge of the bed, not too close together, both of us barely breathing. Sam spoke first.

"You've really got it, don't you?" he asked. I shook my head, not quite sure what he was getting at. "I mean," he explained, "you really are a math genius, aren't you? A prodigy."

"I don't know," I whispered. "I think so. But I try not to think about it too much."

Sam smiled. "So how do you feel about math, then?"

"It's everything," I said, my voice growing stronger. "But I don't know how I feel about that, you know? About feeling that it's everything."

"And where does the oboe fit in?"

"I'm not sure," I said. "It's a hobby, I guess. I

mean, I really like to play, and I plan to stick with it. But math is life. Math is like a passion."

I turned away from Sam, staring into space. "I don't know," I said. "I don't really have the right words for it."

Sam leaned back on the bed and ran his hand through his hair. "You make me feel like an impostor," he said. "I mean, I've done really well and everything, and I've got the grades and test scores to prove it, but I've had to work so hard for it all. You're the real thing."

I didn't know what to say. I had never had this conversation with anyone before, and there I was, baring my intellectual soul to this squeaky clean and sweet and smart guy who just saw me get mugged. My heart was pounding.

Sam threw an arm around my shoulders and pulled me down next to him.

"You're the real thing," he said again, just before we reached out to each other and shared the deepest, most meaningful kiss I had ever experienced in my life. We lay there, side by side, smiling at each other.

"I should study," Sam whispered. I nodded.

"You should," I whispered back. "And I was going to practice."

"I'll come back later," Sam said. "Okay?"

It was more than okay. I kissed him lightly on the nose. "You better."

I must have practiced for hours. I was unaware of time, lost in the music, absorbed in my thoughts. My lips were burning when I finally removed the reed from the oboe. It was dark outside, and I realized that I was hungry.

I wanted to visit Sam. I wanted to slink up to his door as if I really knew how to slink, and sneak into his darkened room. Hello, I wanted to say in my most sultry, experienced voice, how about dinner for two? But, no. Sam was studying, and I was broke. It would be much more dignified, I decided, to settle for ice water until Sam took a study break and came to see me.

There was an ice machine at the end of the hall. I stood in front of it, bucket in hand, trying to will the thing to work. I pressed the red button three or four times. Nothing. Against my better judgment, I stuck my hand up the dispenser.

"That's a good way to get your fingers crushed," a familiar voice said. I spun around. The boy in the black coat took a step backward, startled. He might not have recognized my back, but I never forget a voice.

"What are you doing here?" I was on my toes,

ready to bolt, unsure if I was going to run away from the kid or run straight at him. He relaxed, enjoying my nervousness.

"Glad to see you're feeling better," he said, smiling.

"Get out of here, or I'm calling security." I thought my voice sounded steady and mature. I didn't like it at all when the kid laughed.

"I don't think so," he said.

I didn't know if he was threatening me or not, but I was outraged enough to call his bluff. I stormed past him, close enough to brush up against his coat. He put out his hand to stop me, but withdrew it before actually touching me. I stopped anyway, and stared at him, face to face. He was just a kid, but his brown eyes were old.

"I'm sorry," he said, suddenly serious. "But I'm not going anywhere. I got into a situation outside, so I'm just laying low for a while, okay? I'm not here to bother you, I'm just hiding out until I can leave."

I was not about to get into a conversation with this guy. I walked away from him, toward my room, stopping for just a moment. I had to say something.

"Well, you could at least get off my floor," was what I finally managed to say. Real strong stuff. The kid was more than willing to oblige.

"No problem," he said. He pushed open the door to the stairs and disappeared.

I stopped in front of Sam's room, my hand poised to knock on the door. I watched my fist shake slightly before letting it drop to my side. No way are you going to be the pathetic, scared female, I said to myself. You're fine. Just go back to your room and do some math problems or something.

I guess I was pretty convincing. I went back to my room and flopped on the bed, linear algebra book in hand. But I found myself staring at the ceiling, hating the role of victim and not wanting to play it again.

"Don't be a fool," I said out loud. I reached for the telephone, dialed hotel security, and told them all about the boy in the big black coat.

I read for a while and did a few math problems, but mostly I just daydreamed. I lay on the bed, stretched out on my back, thinking about the day and wondering what the night would bring. I closed my eyes, dreaming of the possibilities and basking in the silence.

I wasn't ready for the screams. They came from outside and pierced the closed window, first one voice, then another, sounds and words I could barely understand, and then there was someone pounding on the door and Sam calling my name, and Sam and Karen rushing in, breathless.

There was a moment of silence. It was the briefest of moments, cut short by a burst of fire from an automatic weapon, and suddenly, I had to know.

"Get the lights!" I said, my voice barely a whisper. Karen obeyed, standing upright and rigid, as if awaiting further orders. I ran to the window, and Sam leaped after me, dragging me back to the center of the room and lying on top of me.

"Are you crazy? Stay down!" He stared at me, the whites of his eyes glistening in the darkness.

But I had to know. I shoved Sam off me, kicking and fighting, and crawled back to the window on my hands and knees, lifting myself up until my eyes were just barely above the sill, and I saw him. I saw him lying facedown on the sidewalk, his body glowing in the harsh light of the street, blood pooling around his head and shoulders. His black coat covered him like a shroud, as if even in death he was still trying to hide.

Sam was on his feet again, grabbing my arms and pulling me back down on the floor, and this time I didn't even try to fight. We huddled together at the foot of the bed, Sam and Karen shaking and gasping for air, and me sitting still and breathing steadily, far past fear and shock and terror, entering a place I had never been before, feeling nothing at all, because I was the only one who knew.

❧

The next morning, when I put my pencil down after filling three blue books, I knew that I would never sit for such an examination again. I remember turning pages rapidly, solving problem after problem, completely confident in the accuracy of every one of my answers. But I do not remember the problems themselves, or the areas of mathematics that they covered, or the adrenaline high I had come to associate with math exams. Something was missing inside, as if a part of me was gone. When it was all over, I knew that I was left with nothing but a perfect score.

I walked back to the hotel alone. Sam and Karen were still in the exam hall, scribbling last-minute answers in their blue books. I knew they were exhausted; all three of us were operating on no sleep at all. The police had paid us a visit late in the night, some time after the murder, but we didn't have anything to say that could be of use to them. Sam did most of the talking, anyway. I just sat on the bed with my back to everyone, staring at the phone.

Sam and Karen caught up with me outside the hotel as I craned my neck to look up at my room window, bloodstains and chalk marks at my feet.

"Come on, Cristina," Sam said, gently taking my arm. "Let's blow this town. I want to forget yesterday ever happened."

I went with him willingly, but I knew it would never be that easy. Yesterday had staked its claim.

I don't really remember getting our bags, or checking out of the hotel, or hailing a cab, but we must have done all of those things. I just remember sitting on a bench in the train station, hugging my oboe close to me, listening vaguely to Sam and Karen talk to an artsy-looking old lady in a black beret.

"How wonderful that you're both going to study at MIT," the old lady said. "And what will you major in once you're there?"

"We don't know for sure, do we, Sam?" Karen answered for both of them. "But it will have something to do with mathematics." I noticed that she was the one holding up their end of the conversation.

Then I felt a hand on my knee.

"And what about you, dear? Will you be joining your friends at MIT?"

"No," I said automatically, without thinking. "I don't know where I'm going to school next year." I knew Sam was staring at me, but I could not feel anything.

"Is there something special that you're planning to do, wherever you go?" The old lady was smiling,

interested. I smiled right back at her, equally interested, because I had absolutely no idea what I was
going to say next.

"I'm going to do what I have always loved best,"
I said, shifting in my seat, closer to the old lady
and away from Sam and Karen. "I'm going to play
the oboe."

A
Good
Deal

THE COURTROOM IS PACKED. MANNY
shifts in his seat, trying to create some distance between himself and the guy on his
left, a scary-skinny, career-felon type, covered with tattoos. He turns to his right,
wanting to talk, but Albert and Jason are staring
straight ahead, barely breathing, like they're in
awe of the judge. They're the best friends a guy
could have, Manny thinks, better than brothers, but
man, are they uptight. Never been to court before,
neither of them. Manny's got one prior, a couple of
years ago when he was still Family Court age. It's
not much, but it's better than nothing.

"Hey," he whispers, elbowing Albert, who jumps in his seat, his trance broken. "How long do you think they're going to make us wait? I got things to do today." Manny grins, like getting arrested is nothing more than an inconvenience, a slight stress on his time. But Albert just shakes his head, and Manny can't tell if that means Albert doesn't know or he's too scared to talk.

"Manuel Riveira!" The judge's voice booms, and Manny can feel it down to the soles of his shoes. He leaps out of his seat like an uncoiled spring.

"Here!" he answers, proud of the strength of his voice, ignoring the peculiar sensation of his legs turning to rubber.

"You're going to Courtroom B, right next door," the judge orders. "Don't move until I call recess."

Manny stands there, waiting. He's got no idea what the judge is talking about; he can't make sense of the words. A dark-haired woman standing in front of the courtroom catches his eye. She points at Manny, then at herself, and then at the door. She holds up an outstretched palm, signaling five minutes. The judge calls Jason next, and Manny sits down quickly. He doesn't even flinch when Tattoo Man's green hand brushes up against his thigh. He pretends not to notice.

❦

An hour passes before the judge finishes calling everyone's names and he finally dismisses them from the courtroom. Manny can't believe it. So much for five minutes. Justice is in no hurry at all.

The same woman who pointed at Manny also wants to talk to Albert and Jason. She's carrying a stack of files when she approaches them in the crowded corridor outside Courtroom B. Manny stares at her, studying her face. Up close, she looks really young—not bad, either. He smiles like he'd smile at her if they met at a party. Bad move. She doesn't smile back. She stares at him until he's ready to give up smiling for the rest of his life. She's a lot tougher than eighteen.

"Good morning," she says, looking none too happy but mercifully breaking the silence. "I'm your public defender. We need to talk. You can call me Cecilia, my last name is too hard to say." Manny's never heard anyone talk so fast in his life. He glances at Albert and Jason. One of them better speak up, because he sure as hell isn't going to open his mouth.

Jason clears his throat. "Excuse me," he cuts in. "You mean you're our lawyer?"

"Right," Cecilia continues. "All three of you got hooked in under the new gambling statute, is that correct?"

She opens a file and flips through it. "Let's see. You were arrested paying off your bookie in the parking lot behind the airport." She smiles suddenly, like she's amused. She looks at Manny. "Sounds like a setup to me. What do you think?"

Manny shrugs like he's got a million more pressing things on his mind.

"I don't know," he says, determined to play it safe. "You're the lawyer."

"That's right. I am." Cecilia keeps on smiling. "Now listen, all three of you. I've already talked to the D.A., and considering you guys seem to be pretty clean kids, she's willing to offer you three months unsupervised probation with your records completely cleared at the end of three months. How does that sound? Good deal?"

Manny doesn't say anything, but for some reason, he trusts her. She talks so fast, she must be a good lawyer. Jason does his throat-clearing thing again.

"So we can go home today and that's it?" he asks.

"Right. Keep your noses clean for three months, and it's like none of this ever happened." Cecilia shifts her files and glances over her shoulder. "I don't want to rush you into anything, but I can't afford to spend too much time on this. I've got some people facing some pretty serious charges who need my attention."

Albert jams his hands into his jeans pockets. "Let's do it," he says. "I mean, let's get out of here." Albert is not having a good time. Manny punches him in the shoulder. The guy needs support.

Jason turns to Manny. "If it's okay with you, it's okay with me, you know what I'm saying?"

Manny nods. No problem.

"Great," Cecilia says. She can't stop smiling now—it's like her day is made. "Go on into Courtroom B and have a seat. You might have to wait a while, but when the bailiff calls your names, come up to the bench. I'll be there. The judge will ask you how you want to plead, and all you have to do is tell him you're pleading guilty. He'll give you your three months probation—unsupervised, so it's nothing, really—and that'll be it." She pauses suddenly. Manny shakes his head. She's amazing. He was wondering when she would need to come up for air.

"Okay? All set?" she asks, diving right back in again. "I'll see you in there. Be patient." She turns to go, ready to focus on all those people facing serious charges.

"Tough break," Jason says as he playfully throws an arm around Manny's shoulders. "How's it feel to plead guilty to something you didn't even do?"

Cecilia stops dead in her tracks, like she just hit a wall. She turns and stands face to face with Jason.

"What did you just say?" She is definitely not smiling. Manny tries to remember the last time he was scared of a girl.

Jason glances at him, confused.

"I just mean," Jason explains, "that Manny's never been involved in our gambling ring. It's just Albert and me and some other guys. Manny came along for the ride in case we needed his help with the bookie."

Cecilia looks at Manny. "You mean you're a fighter, not a gambler?"

Manny shrugs. "Something like that."

"So you were about to go into that courtroom and plead guilty to something you didn't even do?" Her voice drops and she looks almost sad. "I'm sorry," she says. "This is partly my fault. Maybe I should have explained better. But you have to speak up! It's just plain wrong to plead guilty when you're not. What are you afraid of?"

You! Manny wants to scream with all his might, but he knows it's impossible. He shrugs again.

"I thought it would be easier if I just went along with your plan," he says.

"No. There's nothing easy about it. It's wrong." Cecilia sighs, subdued. "Listen, I'm going to enter a not guilty plea for you, and you're going to have to come back next week. Then we'll move for dismissal of your case altogether." She points at Jason and Albert. "You two are both guilty, aren't you?" They nod, almost in unison. "I'll see you all in Courtroom B in a little while, then." She puts her hand on Manny's shoulder and stares straight into his eyes. "And as for you, I'll see you next week as well. I'm counting on it."

"And I'm looking forward to it," Manny says, because he knows she's trying really hard not to smile.

Next week, Cecilia's not smiling. At least, Manny doesn't think she is. He doesn't know for sure because he can't even find her.

She's not in Courtroom B or any of the other courtrooms, and she's not in the corridor. Manny doesn't know where else to look. He slips into Courtroom B and sits down in the last row of seats. Maybe he blew it. Maybe today's the wrong day or he's in the wrong place or it's too early or too late. Maybe no one knows he's there.

"Manuel Riveira!" Okay, so they know he's there. The bailiff gestures to the front of the courtroom. "Come forward, please."

He starts up the aisle, and a man with bushy red hair meets him halfway. The man grabs Manny's arm and whispers into his ear: "Hi. I'm Paul. I'm your public defender."

Manny wants to laugh, but he's afraid he won't be able to stop.

"No you're not," he whispers back, instead. "Where's Cecilia?"

"She's across town doing a felony trial. I'm handling her smaller cases today." Paul looks up at the judge's bench. "Your Honor," he says, "may I have a minute with my client?"

"One minute and only one minute," the judge responds. He does not look happy. "I've got a full docket here."

Manny wants to offer to come back at a more convenient time for everybody, but Paul is pushing him into a chair at a table in front of the bench. Every inch of the tabletop is covered with files. Paul finds the one he's looking for and whips it open. He elbows Manny in the ribs.

"It says in here they offered you three months unsupervised probation. That's a gift! You have to take it."

"But I'm not guilty!" Manny whispers as loudly as he can.

"Come on," Paul says, his voice rising. "In three months you'll be right back to normal. It's a good deal!"

Manny leans back in his chair, trying to slow things down, trying to stay in control, trying to remember how to think. His mind is racing, but it's going nowhere. The judge is staring at him.

"Is there a problem here, Mr. Riveira?" the judge does not exactly ask. Paul grabs Manny's arm again, harder this time.

"It's a good deal," he repeats, as if chanting a mantra. The judge continues to stare.

"Okay. Let's do it," a voice says, and Manny doesn't even remember thinking the words.

It's all over in a minute.

Manny walks out of Courtroom B alone. You're a free man now, he tells himself. You're never coming back here again. Celebrate. Be happy.

But his mind wanders—*three months . . . unsupervised . . . a gift*—and he is not smiling.

There's a crowd standing in front of the elevators. Manny slips his hands into his jeans pockets, ready to wait patiently. He's got no place special to be. All around him, people are in a hurry. It's easy to identify the judges and lawyers, carrying their files and briefcases, but who are all the other people? Are they criminals, or are they just people accused of crimes? Who is guilty and who is innocent?

Manny waits with them, one of the crowd, trying to figure out the difference.

FACING DONEGALL SQUARE

A BOMB WENT OFF IN BELFAST yesterday. The sirens began howling only minutes before the blast, while I stood in the middle of the Gap, of all places, with a pair of jeans draped over my arm, thanking God that I had just got out of the dressing room in time. The sirens I could handle, but being caught with my pants down during a moment of civil crisis might have finished me off.

The salespeople sprang into action, and a woman with a quivering smile snatched the jeans from my hands, promising me that I could pick them up later, whatever that meant. I really liked the way those jeans fit, too. People were trying not to panic, running toward the very same doors that the army, or the police, or whoever the guys with the automatic weapons might be, were charging through.

"Get out! Get out!" the army guys shouted, but I just stood there, somehow convinced that my American citizenship granted me some kind of immunity.

A security guard grabbed me by the shoulders and shoved me toward the door.

"Come on, love, move!" he roared as I turned my face away from him, not wanting him to read in my eyes, in my expression, what I had suddenly realized.

I knew who planted the bomb.

It wasn't my idea to go to Belfast in the first place. I was perfectly content to stay in Dublin with my sister, Allie, who was studying at Trinity College. Allie was the first person in our family to go to college at all, and she wanted to make the most of it by spending her junior year in Ireland. I was supposed to be the second college-bound family member, which was the only reason Mom let me spend spring break with my "positive-influence-on-you" big sister.

I had looked forward to a fun and wild Irish vacation, during which Allie and I would roam the streets of Dublin, on the lookout for poets and musicians. Especially musicians. But Allie had a thesis due that term on some eighteenth-century Irish guy, and, of course, she would settle for nothing less than an honors grade. And the only possible way to earn an honors grade, she said, was to spend a day combing through historical documents at the Public Records Office of Northern Ireland. She actually seemed excited about it.

In any event, three days before I was supposed to return to the States, we caught the 8:00 A.M. train out of Dublin and arrived in Belfast two hours later.

"I'm going to get lost," I said for the seventeenth time, as our black cab stopped in the middle of beautiful, barbed-wired Belfast. The driver laughed. Allie smiled, but I could tell her patience was wearing thin. Allie had presented me with an unusually creative idea moments before our train had pulled into the station. She would do her research alone while I explored the city—also alone. In other words, my sister was ditching me. I was not impressed.

"Look, Julie," Allie said as she rolled down the cab window. "This is City Hall." She pointed to a huge, official-looking building. "This whole block is called Donegall Square. The shopping district is across the street. There are all kinds of restaurants and shops there. Whenever you get confused, just face Donegall Square. I'll meet you there at four. You can't possibly get lost." She sounded totally convinced.

I looked at my sister, with her thick auburn hair and dark eyes. How could two people who look so much alike be so unbelievably different? Allie was the studious type, craving solitude, while I was a true social animal with, by my own admission, something of a tendency to run off at the mouth. I knew Allie was smart to get rid of me if she wanted to get anything done. But no way was I going to let her get away guilt-free.

"Mom's going to kill you when she finds out you took me here," I said. "You know she's got this thing about war-torn cities."

"Come on, Julie, get out," Allie said. "This place is safer than any American city. You'll be fine." I stared at her, convinced that my only sister in the world lacked a soul.

I climbed out of the cab and faced Donegall Square. The driver pulled off, and Allie held up four fingers through the open window. Four o'clock. Just six hours to go. I was overcome with joy.

I shouldn't have been nervous. I mean, I wasn't exactly an experienced world traveler, but I'd been around the proverbial block more than a couple of times. Like most kids from my neighborhood back home, I had seen my share of drugs and guns. I should have been prepared for anything. But my American street bravado disappeared along with my sister. I did not want to be alone.

Any way you look at it, I didn't exactly start out on the right foot. Actually, I did start out on my right foot, glancing quickly to the left as I stepped off the curb. Of course, since I was in Belfast, the traffic was barreling toward me from the right. I froze.

"Watch it, Miss!" a voice called out from behind me. Someone grabbed my arm, yanking me back on the sidewalk.

I liked him immediately. I imagined that I would probably feel a certain degree of affection for just about anyone who saved my life, but I really liked the way this particular hero looked. He was probably a year or two older than I was, maybe even eighteen, but he was wearing one of those school uniforms every high school kid in all of Ireland is required to wear. It made him look younger, and I liked his shaggy hair and easy smile. He shifted his backpack.

"I'd say you're an American," he said. There wasn't a trace of doubt in his voice.

"My stupidity gave me away?"

"No, no! That's not what I meant," he said with a quick laugh. A very nice hand landed on my shoulder. He seemed to appreciate my sense of humor. Definitely a plus.

"On your way to school?" I asked, glancing at his backpack. It looked heavy. "Looks like you had a lot of homework."

"Ah, we always do," he said. "But I don't have a class for another hour or so."

"And I don't have a life for the next six hours. My sister's left me stranded until four."

He picked up the hint. "May I escort you across the street then, Miss?" He offered his arm, gentleman-style. Why be shy? I wrapped my arm around his.

"My name's Julie," I said.

"Mine's Seamus."

It crossed my mind that I just might be in love.

Seamus and I had a fun, if unproductive, time together. I mentioned that I could use a new pair of jeans, so off we went, in search of jeans that would satisfy my cultivated American tastes. We darted in and out of a lot of interesting, offbeat little shops, but all I really wanted was another pair of faded Levi's. Finally, Seamus suggested we take a break and stop for tea.

"Sorry I couldn't help you find what you're looking for," he said. He set down our tray on a table near the cafe window.

"And I'm sorry I kept you for so long," I said. "I think you missed your next class."

"Don't worry about it." Seamus waved his hand. "I can afford to miss a class or two. Especially when the options are so appealing." His eyes actually twinkled. I felt privileged to be there, as a witness.

"Seamus," I said, after a moment. "Do you mind if I ask you a question?" He didn't respond immediately. He poured the tea slowly, then carefully folded his hands in front of him.

"Okay."

I took a deep breath. "Why is there a security guard in the doorway of every shop, and why did they all make a point of watching every move you made?" I spoke quickly. I knew enough about the situation in Belfast to know that I was not asking easy questions.

"Julie, what religion are you?" Seamus asked. His voice was quiet, but clear.

"Catholic," I practically whispered. I felt like I was telling a secret.

"You see this emblem?" Seamus pointed to the chest pocket of his uniform jacket. I nodded. It was pretty hard to miss the purple and gold cross and staff. "That means I'm Catholic, too. And that means that I'm automatically a threat to the national security—or something momentous like that."

I detected at least a trace of bitterness in his voice, but I was struck more by the calmness, the evenness of his tone.

"I'm sorry," I said.

Seamus shrugged. "It's life." He leaned over and kissed me on the cheek. "But I do have to go to my next class," he said. "Physics, you know." He stood up and hoisted his backpack onto his shoulders. I imagined it filled with heavy physics books. He must be brilliant, I thought. I just had to try to see him again.

"I have an idea," I said. "I'm supposed to meet my sister at four in front of City Hall. Do you think you could meet us there and maybe have dinner or something before we have to go back to Dublin?"

Seamus smiled. I really wanted him to say yes.

"I'd love to. I would," he said. "But let me see how the rest of the day goes. If everything goes smoothly, I'll be there. But if something comes up—you know, at school or whatever—I won't be able to make it. You know how it is."

"Believe me, I do," I said. "You can't even imagine how many times I've had to stay after school."

Seamus laughed. "Actually," he said, "I think I probably can." He leaned over again, kissed me on the other cheek, and then, quickly, he was out the door.

I sighed. I glanced at my watch. Four more hours to kill. I decided to hang out in the cafe for a while and relive the last two hours, before heading out to continue my search for a new pair of jeans.

I was surprised when I found the Gap. It was a large, modern building, part of a whole arcade of new stores. It would have been the obvious place to shop for American jeans. I wondered why Seamus hadn't taken me there.

Fifteen minutes later, when I was in the middle of a crowd sprinting up the street away from the sound of a bomb exploding, I didn't wonder anymore.

Idiot! I screamed at myself silently. No high school kid just shows up at school in the middle of the day. No one carries around a backpack that heavy. Everyone knows you can buy American jeans at the Gap. Idiot.

But I knew I was being too tough on myself. Seamus was good, very good. He didn't give me any real clues. We just spent a nice morning together, that's all. Still, call it intuition, I knew Seamus had planted that bomb.

I was the first of the crowd to stop running. Somehow, being able to put a face behind the bomb made me less afraid. And then, suddenly, I was angry. My mind clicked in, sharp, clear, focused. I felt like I was back home, ready to think on my feet. Okay, I thought, he can't be far away. The army had occupied the whole block almost immediately. Seamus had to be hiding somewhere.

I walked up another block before crossing over to backtrack. If I wandered back behind the bombing scene, I might be relatively inconspicuous. And if someone did approach me, I knew I could pull off a little lost American girl routine. I was well aware, however, that if I suspected Seamus was still in the area, the police would, too. I wasn't sure if I cared who found him first.

I almost didn't recognize him when I saw him. I was cutting across a junkyard of sorts, outside the police barriers, and there he was, about twenty yards away, crouched between an abandoned refrigerator and a heap of scrap metal. The backpack was gone, and he was wearing different clothes— jeans and a black sweater—but that wasn't why he looked so different.

His whole being had changed. He seemed shriveled, tiny, his eyes darting left and right, and when those eyes found mine, the nervousness turned to horror. He held up his hands and shook his head. I took a step backward, somehow aware of the danger of my presence.

"Miss! Miss!" a voice called from the distance, and a soldier was running toward me, an automatic weapon slung across his chest, black boots pounding on the pavement. Seamus dove inside the refrigerator, leaving the door open just a crack. I imagined him inside, afraid to breathe deeply, gasping for air.

Now is the time, I commanded myself, and I felt my hand rise to point to the refrigerator.

I waved at the soldier instead.

"Hel-lo!" I called in my most innocent American accent.

The soldier stood in front of me, both hands on his gun. I decided not to see it.

"Can you help me?" I continued. "I'm lost. I'm supposed to meet my sister at City Hall." He studied me carefully, his suspicion turning to disgust.

"What are you doing here, love?" he asked. "This place is dangerous. City Hall is that way." He gestured behind him.

"I'm sorry," I said.

"Move along," he ordered. "Quickly."

I obeyed. I resisted the urge to glance back toward the refrigerator. I smiled at the soldier and turned to face Donegall Square.

Rock
Star

CAT SAID SHE'D NEVER BEEN HIT BY a man before, and she sure as hell didn't expect it to happen for the first time during afternoon detention in Sister Kathleen's homeroom. She said no one ever warned her about tenth-grade English teachers with really cool hair who played the electric guitar. She was actually pretty embarrassed, she said, because she thought she had the situation under control. Cat always thinks she's a step ahead of everyone. Usually she is. But she was wrong about Rock Star, and I knew it. I saw the whole thing coming.

Mr. Paterson could have had it made. On the first day of school, Cat and I and the rest of Mercy High's honors sophomore English class filed into Room 19 and simultaneously fell in love.

"Hey, O'Connor, who broke down and hired him?" Cat breathed into my ear as we slid into our preferred seats in the back of the classroom. The first shock was that the guy sitting behind the teacher's desk was actually a *guy*—thereby doubling the male faculty at Mercy. Then I saw that he was young and his brown hair was pulled back into a small ponytail and he had stubble on his chin and he was smiling. Of course he was smiling. Thirty teenage girls wearing blue plaid skirts and white shirts were sitting in front of him, and twenty-nine of them had their mouths open. Cat's lips were pressed firmly together, betraying only the slightest interest.

Mr. Paterson quickly proved that he was more than just a pretty face. He jumped from his seat, his arms loaded with paperback books.

"Modern drama, women," he said. "That's going to be the focus of our year together. Oh, we'll do all of the regular tenth grade stuff, but we'll spend most of our time reading, discussing, and writing about plays." He paused, waiting for our reaction.

Personally, I had no strong feelings about

modern drama—I was still studying his chin stubble. Very nice.

Suddenly, Mr. Paterson jumped on top of his desk.

"Here!" he shouted, tossing paperbacks around the room. "Read! Get excited! Show some passion!"

We dove out of our seats, trying to catch the books in midair or scooping them up off the floor. This was better than gym class, I thought. Let's face it; so far, this was better than any class. Everyone was talking and laughing, and then I noticed that Cat hadn't left her seat.

Mr. Paterson noticed, too. He leaped from his desk to the first desk in the front row and then from desk to desk until he was standing squarely on top of Cat's, staring down at her.

"Special delivery," he said as he dropped a copy of *Buried Child* into her lap. Cat sat back abruptly, and Mr. Paterson stumbled, regaining his balance just in time.

"Don't fall now," Cat said softly, like she couldn't care less. Mr. Paterson crouched down to get a better look at her and her curly black hair and those green Cat-eyes. Then his forehead crinkled as his whole face broke into a grin, and I knew that Cat had him exactly where she wanted him.

Everyone was jealous. English class was quickly

becoming the Cat and Pat show, as Miranda Kelly put it. Miranda was almost out of her mind with jealousy. She sat in the front row, relentlessly batting her heavily lined eyes at Mr. Paterson, agreeing with everything he said.

Cat sat next to me in the back row and stared out the window all class long. She rarely volunteered a comment or answer, but Mr. Paterson called on her all the time anyway, hanging on her every word. To be fair, Cat did seem to get more out of this modern drama stuff than the rest of us, but I still felt kind of bad for Miranda. She should have gotten something for all her effort. She deserved at least a smile.

Cat got a lot of smiles. Mr. Paterson smiled at her when she walked into class in the morning, he smiled every time he looked at her during class, and he smiled some more when he watched her walk out the door at the end of the period. But the biggest smile I ever saw in my life was on Mr. Paterson's face when Cat and I ran into him at a city bus stop one Saturday afternoon.

The guy was thrilled to pieces. Cat and I were lugging our bassoons home from a Youth Symphony rehearsal when he saw us. My heart stopped when he suddenly appeared right in front of us.

"Good afternoon, women!" he said, his whole face beaming.

The blood started somewhere in my toes and within seconds rushed up my neck to the top of my scalp. I knew I was beet red and my lips were on fire. I hated myself for letting any man have such a drastic effect on my complexion. I glanced at Cat. Nothing. She didn't even flinch.

"How you doing, Mr. Paterson?" she asked.

Mr. Paterson nodded politely at me, but his eyes were on Cat.

"What've you two got in those cases?" he asked. "Machine guns?"

"Bassoons," I answered quickly, surprised I even remembered. "We *are* the Youth Symphony bassoon section."

"Impressive," he said again, nodding in my direction but returning his gaze to Cat. "I'm a musician, too—electric guitar, mostly, although I do bang around with an acoustic. My band plays in clubs all over town." He rubbed his chin stubble. "You should come see us play sometime."

Cat smiled and wrinkled her nose. "Right," she said. "Like we're not way underage."

A bus pulled up to the curb. Mr. Paterson took a step toward it.

"That's mine," he said. Then he stopped abruptly and stepped back toward Cat. He reached out and gently ran his fingers through her hair, caressing her curls. "I've wanted to do that since the first day of school," he said softly.

I almost died. And Cat looked about ready to jump out of her skin, so I knew I wasn't overreacting.

"Good-bye, Rock Star," Cat said almost tauntingly, but her voice was tight, higher than usual. We watched Mr. Paterson board his bus and disappear.

I sat on the curb. Cat sat next to me.

"Miranda Kelly was right," I said after a moment.

"What has Miranda Kelly ever been right about in her life?" Cat asked, her voice back to normal, back in control. But she looked at me like she knew exactly what I was going to say.

"It's obvious," I said. "Mr. Paterson's in love."

"He called me last night."

Cat was leaning against my locker like her head hurt, but she looked pretty pleased with herself. She had been standing there waiting for me first thing Monday morning. A whole day and a half had passed since our bus stop encounter, and we hadn't discussed it any further. It was like we were avoiding the topic, although I wasn't sure why. I decided to play dumb.

"Who?" I asked.

"Rock Star, O'Connor, who the hell else? Although he didn't exactly identify himself." Cat smiled, more to herself than to me. "It was kind of pathetic, really," she continued. "He invited me to go with him to *Buried Child*. It opens at some little theater this weekend."

I opened my locker slowly and pretended to look for something in one of my notebooks. I didn't want to make a big deal out of this, but I couldn't ignore the pit in my stomach.

"You did not say yes," I said.

"Of course not," Cat said. "I just kept saying 'Excuse me? Excuse me?' over and over, until I finally told him I had to hang up. He was babbling about Sam Shepard being his favorite American playwright or something. The whole thing was unbelievably weird. I think he's lost it."

"He's probably totally ill," I said. "But he's been pretty okay in school, though. I mean, English is definitely my favorite class. He's good."

"I know. I think that makes everything even scarier," Cat said, not scared at all. "You know, upstanding Mr. Paterson by day, depraved Rock Star by night. Maybe he's got a thing for teenage girls." She grinned like she was thoroughly entertained.

I slammed my locker shut. No, Rock Star only had a thing for one teenage girl. "Just be careful," I said as I headed off to homeroom. "Don't get in over your head."

My advice was cool, I thought. It was mature. It even made sense—a lot more sense than the scream I felt welling up inside me, trying to call attention to my existence.

Cat didn't get any more phone calls, but Mr. Paterson was all over her in class. Everything she said was brilliant, everything she wrote was worthy of publication, and every thought that crossed her mind had to be expressed. It wasn't Cat's fault, not really. She never even raised her hand to speak. Mr. Paterson asked for comments from a few people, but when he wanted to hear something really worthwhile, he always turned to Cat. Cat thought the whole thing was hilarious, but I think she was the only one.

Then came the day when even Cat stopped laughing. School was over, and there were just a few people still roaming around the building. Cat and I usually took the city bus home, and if we didn't fly out of school the moment the final bell rang, we'd miss the first bus and have to kill a half hour before the next one came. So I was just strolling around the corner to hang out with Cat when I saw her and Mr. Paterson in front of her locker. Mr. Paterson was grinning his face off, of course, but Cat did not look happy.

"Hey, O'Connor," she called. "Come on over here and tell our English teacher that we have a bus to catch."

It seemed like an odd thing to say, but I said it: "We have a bus to catch." I'm sure I promptly blushed bright red. It had become an involuntary reaction in this man's presence.

Mr. Paterson folded his arms across his chest and sort of rocked back on his heels. He wasn't smiling quite so much, but he still looked pretty amused.

"So," he said. "Do you two women do everything together? What are you, in love?"

"Shut up," Cat said, staring at him. She grabbed my arm. "Come on, O'Connor. Let's get the hell out of here."

I didn't say anything until we reached our bus stop. Cat was so mad she was barely breathing.

"Come on, Cat," I finally said. "What was that all about?"

Cat glared off into the distance. "He wanted to give me a ride home."

My heart skipped a beat. There had to be more. "And?" I asked.

"And he wouldn't take no for an answer, okay?" she said quickly. "Just trust me, he got way out of line." She turned toward me for a moment. "You know how I hate this stuff," she said.

To be honest, I wasn't really sure what she meant by "this stuff."

I tried to be supportive. "He's too weird," was all I came up with. Cat nodded, and the conversation was over.

Cat cut English the next day. It was pretty hard to get away with cutting a class at Mercy. I mean, it was like Big Sister was always watching. Mr. Paterson stared at Cat's empty seat and then checked his desk for the absentee list. I knew Cat's name wasn't on it. She was in school, all right, she was just making a statement. Mr. Paterson pressed his lips together until they almost disappeared, forming a thin, red line.

He pointed at me. "Where's your other half?"

I shook my head. "Haven't seen her today," I lied, and my face burned.

Cat showed up in Chemistry next period, and after that we had lunch together in the cafeteria. It wasn't like she was hiding or anything. When Miranda Kelly saw us sitting there at lunch, she tore out of the cafeteria like she was Paul Revere or somebody. I looked at Cat, to see if she noticed.

"What do you think of that?" I asked.

Cat shrugged, but her eyes were on fire. "We'll see," she said. "This could get interesting."

It did. Minutes later, Mr. Paterson stormed into the cafeteria, waving a pink slip. He slammed it down in front of Cat. The whole table shook, and everyone sitting around us was silent as we all watched Mr. Paterson storm back out.

Cat picked up the pink slip. A detention. For cutting English. Mr. Paterson couldn't have made a bigger mistake. Mercy was a pretty detention-happy place, and no one liked it. If there was one issue that united the student body, it was our universal contempt for little pink slips.

"Come on," Cat said, suddenly jumping to her feet. "Let's party."

Someone else brought the radio, but Cat provided the rest of the entertainment. She led us to the basement, to the secluded bathroom near the gym where everyone went who wanted to smoke or drink or worse. A whole bunch of people jammed into the place and watched Cat open the first stall. Moving slowly to the music, she held up the pink slip and carefully tore it into small pieces. She let go of the first piece above the toilet bowl and watched it float gently down into the water. Then, with a flourish, she flushed it away. Everyone cheered. Someone turned up the radio, and we all started to dance. Even me.

Cat traveled from stall to stall, dropping a piece of pink paper into each toilet and flushing them all individually. It was a great performance—modern drama at its best. It seemed only fitting that Mr. Paterson showed up for the last act.

He was with Miranda Kelly. She must have chased after him again, although it was pretty hard to believe that anyone had so little dignity. I reached out to grab Cat, but she had already spotted them. She held up a piece of the detention for Mr. Paterson's benefit and ceremoniously popped it into her mouth. She chewed it slowly before spitting it into the nearest toilet. Then she flushed.

Something happened to Mr. Paterson's face. He didn't seem embarrassed or angry; he just looked kind of . . . different. Strange. Hard. The stubble on his chin looked like a million little daggers about to shoot out. And for the first time since I met him, I didn't feel myself turning red or getting hot. If anything, I was cold.

"Be careful," I whispered suddenly to Cat, and this time I meant it, although I couldn't have explained why.

"He's nothing," Cat said. "Don't worry about Rock Star."

Mr. Paterson disappeared, followed by Miranda, and all I could do was worry.

The "flushing party," as it came to be called, was big news the next day. Even some seniors stopped Cat in the halls, congratulating her on the success of the event. Cat was in a pretty good mood all morning, especially when I agreed to cut English with her. We hung out in the gym locker room just talking and relaxing, and then we decided that there was nothing wrong with cutting Chemistry, too. The worst thing that could happen would be to get a detention from Sister Kathleen, our chemistry teacher. We also decided, ahead of time, that if Sister Kathleen did give us detentions, we would comply, no questions asked. We didn't have a problem with her.

So Cat and I stayed in the locker room until the bell rang for first lunch. We were on our way to the cafeteria when we stopped at Cat's locker.

Cat opened her locker door and turned toward me, all the color drained from her face.

"There's a doll in my locker," she said.

I looked inside. Sitting on the top shelf of Cat's locker was a plastic little girl, naked and filthy, like it had just been dug up out of the ground. That was sick enough for me, but the worst part was the doll's head. It was on backwards, tilted at a crazy angle, as if someone had twisted her neck.

Before I could say anything, Cat grabbed the doll

and sprinted into the cafeteria. I raced after her, just in time to see her rush up to Miranda Kelly and shove that doll in Miranda's face.

"Do you know anything about this?" Cat shouted.

Miranda shrieked and leaped out of her seat. She grabbed the doll and threw it to the floor. Then she called Cat crazy and Cat called her crazy and Miranda dumped her diet soda all over Cat and Cat pushed her into a table and then, of course, a crowd gathered around them.

That's when I picked up the doll and took a good look at it.

"Cat," I said, softly at first, but then repeating her name, louder and louder. "Cat, Cat, *Cat*." I shoved my way to the center of the crowd, between Cat and Miranda.

I held up the doll. "Buried child," I said, and they both stared at me.

"Oh, my God," Miranda whispered. "Oh, my God."

Then Cat started to say it, too: "Oh, my God...oh, my God." And then they were staring at each other, and Cat knew that Miranda wasn't crazy, and Miranda knew that Cat wasn't crazy, either.

But we all knew who was.

The next day, Sister Kathleen presented pink slips to both Cat and me. She tried to make it easy on us since we had never given her any trouble before.

"Why don't you two help me clean up my homeroom today after school," she offered. "We'll call it even, and you won't have to attend a formal detention period."

The day passed quickly enough, especially since Cat and I cut English again. Cat didn't seem too concerned, but I couldn't help but worry when Mr. Paterson would make another move. I mean, we were dealing with a crazy person. Besides, there was no way he could allow our little boycott to last much longer and still maintain Mercy High's strict disciplinary standards. But the final bell rang, ending another day, and he still hadn't come looking for us.

"Ready to scrub blackboards?" Cat asked when I met her outside Sister Kathleen's homeroom.

"Here," I said, handing Cat my books. "Take these inside for me. I just need to run to the bathroom."

I wasn't gone long, five minutes at the most, but when I got back no one was scrubbing blackboards.

Mr. Paterson and Cat were standing on opposite sides of the teacher's desk, staring each other down. Cat looked cornered, but she smiled when she saw me.

"What's going on?" I asked, practically spitting the words. "Where's Sister Kathleen?"

"Something came up. I'm subbing," Mr. Paterson said, still staring at Cat.

I took a couple of steps toward them, and Cat walked around the desk in my direction, stopping just a few feet away from Mr. Paterson.

"It looks like it's two against one now, Rock Star," she said, and that's when he hit her.

He didn't slap her or anything, although that would have been bad enough. He absolutely hauled off and slugged her. Cat dropped like she had been shot. I froze, and my mind clouded over. This is nothing like television, I thought. On television, people stagger around and travel great distances before falling. In real life, they crumple. I wondered why. Then Mr. Paterson's voice cut through my haze.

"It's back to one-on-one now, honey," he said. He made a move in my direction, and I bolted across the room and grabbed the window pole. I didn't even remember seeing it, but it suddenly occurred to me that a long window pole with a hook at the end could make one hell of a weapon.

I swung at him. I missed. I didn't mean to hit him, really, but I had to do something. The window pole crashed into the side blackboard, cracking it from top to bottom.

Out of the corner of my eye, I saw Cat get to her feet, holding her jaw.

"Get out of here, Rock Star," she said, her voice sounding pained, but clear.

Mr. Paterson didn't even look at her. He backed up toward the door. He was staring at me.

"Not bad for a Catholic-school girl, O'Connell," he said. "I didn't think you had it in you." He sauntered out of the room.

I paused for a moment, and then, still clutching the window pole, I ran out into the hall just in time to watch Mr. Paterson turn the corner.

"It's O'Connor!" I shouted after him, even though I knew it no longer mattered.

We never saw Mr. Paterson again. I think the official story was something about a crisis in his family and having to take a job closer to home. Cat said nothing to cast any light on the situation. It was her choice.

"No one finds out about this, okay, O'Connor?" she said after the emergency-room doctor wired her jaw. He bought the story about her taking a baseball in the face, and I guess everyone else did, too. That's the way Cat wanted it.

Things got back to normal pretty quickly at Mercy. An older nun called Sister Matilda was dragged out of retirement to teach us Shakespeare, who was probably her idea of a modern playwright.

Miranda Kelly and Cat actually smiled and nodded whenever they saw each other. And Cat and I grew closer, like we had somehow reached a new level of understanding.

But there was something I did not understand, something that haunted me around the middle of every school day when I met up with Cat at her locker. Every day, Cat would swing open her locker door, drop off her books, and grab her lunch, all the while talking about something completely ordinary. And every day, I would fake my way through the conversation, smiling and acting totally normal, determined not to return the glassy stare of the naked, filthy doll sitting on the top shelf of Cat's locker.

IMMORTALITY

I WAS ONLY FOURTEEN AT THE TIME and couldn't drive, otherwise I would have been at the wheel, I was sure of it. My mother always said that I had more nerve than brains, and everyone knew I had a lot of brains. My sister, Sandra, who was driving, still remembers how I put my hand on that cop's gun while he was wearing it in his holster. I just put my hand on it, and he put his hand on top of mine. I wasn't even scared, though Sandra, who was thirteen then, almost died. You don't mess with cops, she still says. But I just smiled up at him, and he took his hand off mine and put it on top of my head like he was going to mess up my hair. I let him keep it there for a couple of seconds before I ducked away. It wasn't like I cared about my hair or anything. It's thick and black and tough to mess up.

But even my hair was really messed up that night in Sandra's car. We had all the windows open, and Sandra was driving so fast that I wouldn't have been surprised if my hair blew right off. Sandra's friend Laura was screaming her head off in the backseat, but I knew she was loving it because we were winning. We were beating the guys. Mikey and Tony were gaining on us over in the left lane, but they were stuck. They'd never make the exit from there.

It was time for us to cut over, and as I slapped both hands against the dashboard, Sandra swore out loud in Italian and swerved neatly across two lanes. The guys shot past us on the left as the Gano Street sign disappeared over our heads. Then we heard the sirens. We had been speeding our brains out all the way from Newport since I had suggested we make a race out of the ride back to Providence, and it was some kind of miracle that we hadn't seen any cops the whole way. Until now. The cops whipped past us as we slowed down heading toward the exit ramp. They were chasing Mikey and Tony, and I hoped those guys knew enough to let themselves get caught.

The race was over. The China Inn was less than ten minutes away doing the speed limit. It would have been a lot more fun to screech into the parking lot, neck and neck with the guys, but I knew they'd make it eventually, with a lot to say. I thought about General Tso's chicken with broccoli and rice. . .and Mikey snuggling up next to Sandra, but saving a wink for me.

We decided to hang out in the parking lot and wait. My cousin, Tina, climbed out of the backseat and slammed the door. I had almost forgotten she was with us, with all the wind blowing and Laura screaming and sirens wailing. She didn't say a word but stared straight at me, her eyes looking like two big black olives, the kind with the pits already out.

Why did she have to look at me like that when she knew I was the youngest and not responsible? Everyone else was at least two years older than me, and no one was stupid. I think, at that moment, I hated her, but even then I didn't really know why. She wasn't the only one with big, dark eyes. And she wasn't the only one thinking about death.